A Prior
ENGAGEMENT

A PRIOR ENGAGEMENT

Larkhall Letters Novella

ASHTYN NEWBOLD

THREE LEAF
PUBLISHING

Copyright © 2022 by Ashtyn Newbold

All rights reserved.

No part of this book may be reproduced in any form or by any electronic or mechanical means, including information storage and retrieval systems, without written permission from the author, except for the use of brief quotations in a book review. Any references to historical events, real people, or real places are used fictitiously. Names, characters, and places are products of the author's imagination.

ISBN: 9798367129267

Cover design by Ashtyn Newbold

Three Leaf Publishing, LLC

www.ashtynnewbold.com

CHAPTER 1

Perhaps it wasn't wise to exchange her hand in marriage for a puppy, but Julia couldn't withdraw from the bargain now. It was in writing, and she held the very letter in her hand. She would miss that puppy, but one day, when she was Oliver Northcott's wife, it wouldn't matter. The puppy would be hers again anyway.

She grinned to herself. She had always considered herself to be quite intelligent for the age of eleven, but now she could see that she was just plain clever.

"It's time to sign the agreement," Julia said, planting one hand on her hip as she turned toward Oliver. He chewed his lower lip nervously.

Her friend Mary had joined her to be the witness of Oliver's signature on the letter. It had taken less than two minutes to draft the specifics of their bargain, and

Julia could confidently say that everything was done according to her own wishes.

"If I sign this now, then we are as good as engaged." Oliver glanced up, blue eyes filled with skepticism. Boys at the age of eleven were never quite as clever as the girls. But that was the problem. Oliver was twelve.

He studied the page one more time, brow furrowing. His blond hair shone like golden biscuits in the early morning sunlight. Julia had instructed him and Mary to meet near the edge of his family's property where their parents wouldn't find them and see what they were up to. The estate of Larkhall was grander than any Julia had ever seen. It wouldn't be Oliver's, for he had an elder brother, but that was a sacrifice she was willing to make. Surely he would find a respectable profession in the clergy or military or something like that.

There were more important matters to consider, such as love. And Julia was in love with Oliver Northcott. She didn't care who told her that eleven was too young to be in love. She was clever enough to recognize what those flutters in her stomach and blushing of her cheeks meant. If she couldn't go a day or even an hour without thinking of him, smiling about something he said, then how could she not be in love with him?

"You are being silly, Oliver," Julia said. "We are too young to be engaged."

"If I sign this, promising to one day marry you,

then we *would* be engaged." Oliver grimaced, his freckled nose scrunching.

Julia sighed. "I told you. My future marriage is all my mama will ever speak about. It is very important, you know, and I must not disappoint her. You must promise in this letter that you will marry me so my future may be secure. I cannot fail my mother and never find a husband. If I have this secured now, then I shall never have anything to worry about."

Oliver hesitated for a long moment, holding his quill against his lips. He squinted up at her from where he sat on the grass with the agreement spread on one of his knees.

"Do you want the puppy or not?" Julia asked, gesturing at Mary, who held the pug against her collarbone. Not only was Mary there to witness Oliver's signature, but she was also there to deliver the puppy. Each step needed to be as official as possible, and Mary was the sort of friend who would participate in such a strange scheme even if she thought it was, well, rather strange.

"Of course I want the puppy," Oliver said, scratching his head. His normally jovial expression was knit with concern. He looked up at Julia again, tipping his head to one side as he studied her. Another grimace twisted his lips. "But what if I don't want to marry you when I grow up?"

She glared at him. "Then you don't get a puppy now." She started to walk away, waving Mary forward.

It was a risk to do so, because she didn't know whether or not Oliver would stop her. In the worse case, she would keep the puppy and attempt to trick Oliver into becoming engaged to her some other way. She did love the puppy a great deal. Her father had bred their dog Millie and she had whelped a litter of six puppies. Papa had already sold three of them, but he had given one to Julia and one to each of her two brothers, giving them the choice to sell their puppy and use the money as they pleased, or to keep it.

"Wait!" Oliver's voice brought a smile to Julia's cheeks.

She brushed a curl from her forehead, turning to face him. "Yes?"

Oliver had forgotten to tuck his shirt in completely on the right side and the left, so the stiff white fabric stuck out both sides like a bicorn hat. "I think I should like to add a provision," he said. "I do not understand why you are so concerned about never finding a husband if you haven't even tried. I think it is only fair that you try first, and if you fail, then I will fulfill this promise. At what age do most ladies marry?"

"Usually within their first season or two, I suppose." Julia shrugged. "That is what my mama wants for me. Perhaps the age of nineteen would be a reasonable age."

Oliver bit his nails as he read the letter again. Julia studied him. Love was a peculiar thing. She couldn't quite understand why she was so fond of this nail-biting boy with a bicorn hat-shaped shirt hem, but when his blue eyes met hers again, her stomach still flipped and flopped. Oliver didn't seem to know she liked him so much. He thought this was all just a way for her to ensure she was married to *someone*. But the truth was, she wasn't interested in marrying anyone unless it was Oliver. It didn't seem possible that her feelings would change. Not so long as she knew him and saw him in town every week.

"Let us revise the agreement to say that if you are not yet married to someone else in ten years, then I will marry you."

"Ten years?" Julia said with a frown. "I will be twenty-one."

"Yes. So that gives you two years past the age of nineteen to try a little harder to find a different husband."

Julia tapped her chin. Well, perhaps that *was* fair. And it could easily be manipulated. She didn't have to accept any proposals she received before that age. "Very well," she said. "Let us add the provision and sign it before Mary has to return home."

Julia threw a sneaky smile at her friend. Mary's large brown eyes gleamed with mischief. Soon their endeavor would be a success. Julia took the pug from Mary's arms, nestling it against her chest. The little whelp was only eight weeks old, and she would miss him terribly. "I do hope you live past the age of ten," she whispered into his floppy ears. "Then you shall be mine again."

She stroked his fur and pressed a kiss to his flat nose before handing him back to Mary.

"Shall I add the provision myself?" Oliver asked, dipping the quill in the carefully balanced inkwell that sat on a rock beside him.

"Yes, and then I'll read it to ensure I approve." Julia read over his shoulder as he wrote what they had discussed. When he finished, she picked up the document and read over the entire thing, giving a concise nod. "You must sign it now."

Oliver glanced at the puppy, a furrow still on his brow, as if he were questioning the wisdom of the idea. Julia held her breath. In truth, she was beginning to question it herself. She bit her lip.

Did she really wish to wait until she was twenty-one to marry? That was what she would have to do. She couldn't possibly marry anyone else at seventeen like Mama had married Papa if she knew that Oliver was required to marry her in just a few years. Yes, Julia would wait for him. She would have waited even longer if she had to.

A slow smile spread over Oliver's face as he lifted the quill once again, a smile that made Julia's heart patter just a little quicker. "This is mad," Oliver said. "I do hope that dog is well-behaved."

"Indeed, he is." Julia patted the puppy's head. "Your mother will surely adore him once she comes to know his gentle disposition." Oliver's mother was not fond of dogs, and so she had not given Oliver any money with which to purchase one himself. If he brought home this pug without having spent a penny, hopefully she would allow him to keep it.

"I think so, too." Oliver gave an eager smile, seeming to forget his anxiety for long enough to sign his name on the document.

"Wait for the witness," Julia instructed, ushering Mary forward. Mary put on the spectacles she had sneaked from her father's study. She looked far more official that way. Holding them to her eyes, she leaned down to properly see the paper.

In a neat and careful hand, Oliver signed his name.

Julia did her best to hide the grin on her face. If Oliver hadn't been watching, she and Mary likely would have squealed with delight, but she couldn't have her future husband thinking her a silly girl. From that moment forward, she needed to act like an elegant lady. If he wasn't in love with her yet, she had ten long years to change that.

Kneeling on the grass, Julia took the paper and signed her own name beside his. As soon as the ink dried, she picked the paper up by one corner, reading it over one last time before giving a nod of approval. "I shall keep this safe for the next ten years, should I need to use it if I am twenty-one and still unmarried."

Oliver didn't seem to hear what she had said. He was reaching for the puppy, snatching it from Mary's arms. His grin was pure delight, eyes bright with excitement. "What shall I name him?" he asked.

Julia stared at the puppy, already missing his velvet fur and wrinkled skin. "I already named him if you would like to use the name I have chosen. His name is Rupert."

Oliver tapped his chin. "I suppose I like that name. He must be already accustomed to being called by it, after all. I should hate to confuse him." He began walking away, his long, lanky legs carrying him across the grass toward Larkhall, not giving her another second of attention. She watched little Rupert's head bobbing as Oliver broke into a run.

Julia looked down at the paper in her hands, stroking the edges with a grin. She didn't need a puppy when she had something far better.

She had Oliver Northcott.

CHAPTER 2

TEN YEARS LATER

Edged in frost, Larkhall looked different than Oliver remembered it. His body swayed with the movements of his coach, but his muscles were limp. Pain throbbed all over his body, despite the long hours in the cold carriage that he had hoped would numb it. His thoughts had been heavy and even colder than the crystals of ice that gathered on the edges of the windows of his childhood home.

He felt nothing as the coach pulled into the courtyard. At least nothing he would have *expected* to feel, knowing that he would soon see his family again after two years away from them. He wasn't eager to jump out of the coach and run inside—he would have rather hidden in the cold than face them as a failure.

He flinched as his shoulder bumped against the side of the door. He had too many injuries to keep track of. Something was sure to hurt with every single movement.

When the conveyance finally came to a halt, he stepped cautiously onto the flat stone of the courtyard. Candlelight flickered through only two of the windows, glaring down at him like a set of disapproving eyes. What would Mother think when she saw him? What of his elder brother Matthew? His younger sister, Bridget? He stopped himself, taking a deep breath to calm the turmoil in his chest. He knew his family. They were kind, generous, and loving. They always had been. He knew, deep in his bones, that they would welcome him home happily, broken or not.

The rest of society…well, of them he couldn't be so certain.

Under usual circumstances, Julia quite enjoyed spending Christmastime in the country. Her family's country house was warm, spacious, and separated from the chaos of London. It was her home, the place she had been raised.

And it was close to Larkhall.

She had always loved how Larkhall looked in the snow, much like a golden biscuit topped with icing. Each year, she treasured December as her last month before preparing to enter London society again with her mother urging her to find success in the marriage mart. December was always the month she could rely on to be free of unwanted suitors.

This year, however, she had not been so fortunate.

"You look like a rose," a sultry voice said from behind her ear.

She didn't turn around for fear of seeing Lord Belper's wet smile far too close to her face. He licked his lips far too often, particularly when he was looking at her.

"I have always liked when women wear my favorite color," came his voice again. "Red."

Julia's stomach lurched, and she walked a little faster down the corridor toward the dining room. Mama had invited Lord Belper to dine with them twice within the last week alone. Not only that, but she had welcomed him into their drawing room to call upon Julia every day for a fortnight. The man was persistent, and so was Mama. Julia couldn't quite determine why her mother was so insistent that she marry Lord Belper, but it had been her ambition from the moment he first paid Julia special attention at the Radcliffes' ball. He was wealthy beyond reason, and his face was moderately handsome. His character, however, was quite odd.

Ignoring Lord Belper never seemed to work. In fact, it seemed to encourage him. He caught up to her as they reached the dining room door. "Miss Reeves, I must confess that I would find you lovely in any color. I daresay you could not go amiss. Well, aside from green. I have never liked when women wear green."

"Thank you, my lord," Julia muttered when her mother cast her a scolding frown. They entered the dining room and were seated in the same arrangement as last time—with Julia directly beside Lord Belper. She breathed deeply, careful not to let her anxiousness overwhelm her. The dining room walls seemed to be closing in, threatening to pin her against Lord Belper forever. That was what would happen if she married him. She would be forever tied to him, and forever uncomfortable.

She had become quite skilled at deflecting suitors in her last two seasons in London. What was another?

She remained cold and still throughout the first course of the meal, offering only brief answers to Lord Belper's incessant questions. His dark hair came to a curl on his forehead, and his eyes glistened in the candlelight as he ate his meal at an alarming rate.

Mama smiled at him as though he were the most intriguing man in the world. He might have been the most intriguing man in the room, but that was because he was the *only* man in the room. Julia's father had been away for weeks on some business matter, leaving the house precisely how Mama liked it. To herself. She could host whatever she pleased, and Julia and her two younger sisters were forced to attend the many social events Mama thought to invent for the Christmastide that year. Julia far preferred the Christmastide traditions of her father, which usually included hiding from all members of society surrounding a burning yule log, greenery, and all the plum pudding he could fit in his belly.

Julia continued to ignore Lord Belper as best as she could, earning several glares from Mama throughout the meal. Determination rose in Julia's chest in response to her mother's resistance. She would do nothing that could be mistaken for encouragement. She didn't wish to mislead any man into thinking she would consider him. Because she was most certainly not considering Lord Belper.

When it came time for the ladies to remove to the drawing room, Lord Belper stayed behind alone to enjoy his port in the dining room. Knowing how much he enjoyed staying at Julia's side, she doubted he would remain at the table for long.

The moment they entered the corridor, Mama found Julia, wrapping her fingers around her elbow. Her golden curls were tight against her temples, sharp blue eyes filled with frustration. "Julia. You cannot be so cold toward Lord Belper."

"I don't wish to mislead him." Julia stopped in the

drawing room doorway, turning to face Mama. "You cannot be serious in thinking that I would marry him."

"I am serious. Very." Mama's eyebrow arched. "Stop being aloof. This could very well be your last chance."

"What do you mean?" Julia scrunched her brow in confusion. "I'm going to London in the spring."

Mama closed her eyes, releasing a slow breath. She lowered her voice. "We cannot afford another season for you. I know you have been planning on a third, but since you failed your first two, the expense might not be worth the reward. Your father must keep funds in reserve for your younger sisters who might take marriage more seriously than you have." Mama's eyes flashed with accusation. "Lord Belper is a respectable and titled gentleman who is in love with you. No woman of sense would reject an offer from him."

Julia sighed, turning away from Mama's censure. In truth, Julia had lost her sense a long time ago. Ten years ago, in fact. And she had never found it again. She could still remember the day Oliver left to work aboard a ship. She had never seen him smiling with so much pride and excitement. She remembered the ache in her heart when she realized that she might not see him for years, and that he had likely forgotten all about their bargain. If he was miles away, floating atop the waves, he couldn't possibly marry her. At least not anytime near her twenty-first birthday, which was approaching in just a few days.

Could she wait for him forever? Their arrangement had been made when they were children. She laughed at it now. She and Oliver had even laughed about it together when they had become a little older and realized how ridiculous it was. But now, faced with Lord Belper's looming proposal, she couldn't help but take that bargain seriously.

"Surely there are other gentlemen I could meet here in Croftstead," Julia said, facing Mama with a lifted chin. "We have family members in other towns and counties as well whom I might visit and be introduced to eligible gentlemen. Lord Belper cannot be my last chance." Julia's voice squeaked in dismay.

Mama opened her mouth to speak again, but stopped when Julia stooped down to pick up the little old dog who waddled out of the drawing room. Rupert had been napping by the fireplace. His squished nose and wrinkled skin were covered in flecks of gray. She hoisted him into her arms, giving his head a pat. Each time she saw the dog, her heart immediately stung. It wasn't a painful sting though—it was a pang of fondness and hopelessness, all muddled together.

It was what she felt each time she thought of Oliver.

He had left Rupert with her when he left for sea two years before. Julia hadn't known if it was his way of trying to discredit their bargain or if he simply knew how much Julia loved the dog.

Mama's serious demeanor faded just as Julia had hoped. She had a softness in her heart for Rupert—one that Julia was often envious of. Mama would have never forced Rupert to live with anyone as horrendous as Lord Belper. No, Rupert's heart belonged to Oliver, and Mama knew it. That was why Julia liked the dog so much. They had a great deal in common.

Scratching behind the dog's ears, Mama let out a sigh. "I wonder if Oliver Northcott will ever return for this dog."

Julia's heart gave a thud at the mention of his name, one she was certain Rupert could feel as she clutched him to her chest. "Unfortunately Oliver Northcott is aboard a ship somewhere very far away."

Lord Belper's unexpected voice made her jump. "No, he isn't."

She turned around slowly. He stood in the dark corridor, head tipped to one side as he observed Julia and her mother standing in the drawing room doorway. After recovering from the fright he had given her, the meaning of his words settled into her skin. "What did you say?"

Lord Belper appeared pleased to have finally struck a subject that captured Julia's interest. "Haven't you heard the news?" He glanced between Mama and Julia, eyes wide. "The Northcott family has always been rather private, I suppose. But I heard in town just yesterday evening that Oliver, the younger son, has just returned from his ship after sustaining a few rather serious injuries. I daresay he will not be returning to sea again."

Julia's breath became solid in her throat. She pulled Rupert closer, clinging to some small piece of reality. This couldn't be true. Oliver couldn't really be back already. Her heart hammered with concern. "Injuries?"

"Yes, I'm afraid so. I have not heard how dreadful it is, but the surgeon and physician have both been seen on the grounds of Larkhall in recent days." Lord Belper licked his lips as his eyes raked over her. "I hope I have not offended your sensibilities by speaking of...*injuries*."

"No." Julia swallowed. "You have not." Her mind raced as she considered what could have happened to Oliver. Dear, sweet, cheerful Oliver. What had the war done to him? Dread flooded her chest.

"His career has ended before it truly began," Lord Belper said. "It is quite tragic. Thankfully his family has enough wealth to sustain him while he seeks a different path. His elder brother Matthew is known for his generosity."

"Yes, of course." Though Oliver had been absent, Julia had still seen the other members of the Northcott family frequently over the last two years. She suspected Matthew knew of her attachment to Oliver, but he never teased her about it. Even if he knew about the attachment, no one besides Julia, Oliver, and Julia's friend Mary knew about the marriage agreement they had both signed all those years ago.

The timing of Oliver's return to Larkhall sent a shiver over her spine. He could save her from Lord Belper. Sudden nervousness boiled in her stomach. She couldn't approach Oliver with that ridiculous piece of paper after ten years, and two years without even speaking to him. He had plenty to worry about besides being trapped into a marriage. That was her own worry to undertake. If Mama had her way, then Julia would be trapped into a marriage of her own with a man she didn't love within a matter of weeks. She couldn't do the same to Oliver.

Her heart flooded with too many emotions to keep track of, beating wildly as she stroked Rupert's head. Was Oliver all right? How injured was he? He was still alive, and that was all that mattered to her. She stared blankly at the floor, completely unaware of the conversation around her. Had Lord Belper asked her a question?

"Julia." Mama's voice broke through the fog, muffled and quiet. "Julia!" Her fingertips pressed into Julia's arm. "Are you all right?"

The dog wriggled in her arms, serving to bring Julia back to her senses. "Yes. Forgive me. I was distracted." Her brow settled into a furrow again.

"Thank you for the information, my lord," Mama said. "I suppose we will have to visit the Northcotts to express our well-wishes to Oliver. Poor man."

Rupert must have sensed Julia's distress, for his wriggling had led him to reposition himself in her arms, just enough so that he could look up at her face.

She met Rupert's round brown eyes, her stomach sinking.

There was one thing that could bring a little joy to Oliver during such a difficult time, and she could not be selfish and withhold it.

She had to return the dog to him.

CHAPTER 3

There were few things Oliver felt fortunate about of late, but one of them was his timing. He stared out the window at the snow that had been falling all day. It was now piled on the windowsill and grass, spiraling through the sky in angry gusts. If he had arrived at Larkhall any later, he might have been caught in the snow. Instead, he was in his bedchamber with a warm fire and cup of tea.

He raked a hand over his hair, careful to avoid the small cuts on his forehead. In the glass of the window, he could see the gash that trailed from his eye down to the bottom of his jaw. The stitches were almost ready to be removed. They had been haphazardly placed by the surgeon on the ship, but there had been many other injured midshipmen to attend to, so the process had been rushed. The scar already showed the result of that.

The more pressing issue, however, was his hand. He

looked down at the bundle of bandages where two of his fingers used to be. He had been doing all he could to combat the pain in his shoulder and leg, and he did have hope that those injuries would recover in time, but he knew for a fact that fingers did not grow back.

He pressed his forehead against the cool condensation on the window, letting it soothe the recovering cuts on his skin. He closed his eyes for several seconds, and when he opened them again, he frowned. His mind was likely fooling him, but he thought he saw a fleck of color out in the snow.

It was moving.

He rubbed his eyes, blinking hard. His vision came into focus. That fleck of color was red, a stark contrast, like a drop of blood in the snow. He shook his head against the morbid comparison. It was a woman in a red cloak, trailing through the snow on foot. And she was headed straight for the front doors of Larkhall.

From his vantage point, he couldn't see her face. Her hood was pulled up on her head to shield her from the snow. Even so, she must have been freezing. Not only that, but she was unaccompanied, unchaperoned, and—

His eyes flew open as she slipped, landing flat on her back. He pushed away from the window instantly, rushing out of his room and down the stairs as quickly as his sore leg would carry him. He still wore his boots, so he didn't have to waste a second as he hurried out the front door to the woman's aid. What the devil was she thinking? Oliver gritted his teeth as he limped across the grass, already regretting his hasty flight down the stairs. His knee screamed at him, but he ignored it.

As he came closer to the woman, he realized she was speaking. Her soft voice cooed like a bird. Had she seen him? Her hood was still pulled down over her eyes, and she was turned away from him, so it didn't seem likely that she was addressing him. "Oh, dear, are you all right?" Her arms surrounded something that moved inside her cloak. Was it...a child? Oliver's eyes widened.

"I'm sorry," she said to the bundle. "I didn't see the ice. You must be so very cold. Not to worry. We are almost there."

Oliver froze, his heart leaping to his throat. He recognized that voice. If his knee was weak already, it was now utterly useless. He couldn't take another step closer, not with the turmoil raging in his chest. He swallowed against his dry throat, managing to find his voice for a brief moment. "Julia?"

Her head jerked up, causing her hood to fall back from her bonnet. Color flooded her cheeks, matching the red tip of her nose. "Oliver." The sound of his name on her voice sent a spiral of memories through his head. He had been trying very hard to forget her for the last two years, but it seemed the task of forgetting someone who was such a prominent part of his life was rather impossible, especially when it came to Julia. And now he saw why it would have been wise to forget her.

She appeared to be holding a child, bundled inside her cloak.

Had she really married so quickly after he left for sea? He had known in his heart that she would. He couldn't imagine how there could be any man in all of England who wouldn't fall in love with her. As her eyes searched his face from her place on the ground, he became suddenly self-aware. She had seen the stitches running down his cheek and the bundle of bandages around his hand. Concern knit her brow. And worse—pity.

He walked forward, unable to hide his limp. A scowl furrowed his brow. "What are you doing out here in the snow?" He found it difficult to look at her face as he reached down to take her hand. He tugged her to her feet, eyeing the moving bundle behind her cloak once again.

Her surprise was evident as she stared up at him. "I might have expected a warmer greeting than that," she said in a quiet voice.

Oliver met her gaze. He still remembered the first day he had noticed the color of her eyes. She had been taunting him in a game of cards when they were fourteen or fifteen years old. She had been leaning across the card table at Larkhall, spouting all sorts of nonsense about how he had cheated and she was the true winner. He had agreed with her. He had *agreed* with her because her eyes had been so blasted pretty and honey-brown and he had been distracted.

Oliver would have to have a word with her husband. How had he left her to walk to Larkhall with their child in her arms, no less? They could have both been injured severely by the fall Julia had just taken. His sour mood did not improve as she patted the wriggling lump in her cloak. "Hold still, my dear," she whispered.

"I'm sorry," Oliver said. "I was concerned. It's far too cold out here. Come inside." He led Julia by the arm, steadying her until they reached the front doors. He shut the doors behind them, closing them off from the wind. The house was quiet and still, the opposite of how Oliver felt inside. He drew a heavy breath, turning to face Julia again. "Are you hurt?"

"No, only embarrassed," she said with a light laugh. Her face was still pink.

He eyed her cloak. "Is the child hurt?"

Her eyebrows shot upward. "Child?"

He cleared his throat, gesturing at the movement under her cloak.

She pressed her lips together, hiding a smile. Before he could embarrass himself further, she unwrapped the top of her cloak, revealing a face that Oliver had never seen on a child before.

A canine face, one with a squished nose and flecks of gray in its fur.

The dog's large brown eyes turned to Oliver, and its ears lifted. It was not a child at all. It was Rupert.

The dog whined, squirming out of Julia's arms. She helped him to the floor, letting the old dog race toward

Oliver, tail wagging vigorously. Relief flooded through Oliver's heart, only half of it being that Rupert was still alive. The other half was entirely dedicated to the fact that Julia did not have a child.

"Rupert, my boy!" Oliver smiled, cringing at the way the expression stretched at the cut on his cheek. The pug ran in a mad circle around his legs until Oliver managed to grab him, scooping him up into his arms. His heart swelled with momentary joy as he held Rupert to his chest.

"I think he missed you," Julia said.

Oliver glanced up from the dog, letting his gaze settle on Julia's face. She appeared just as nervous as he was, her feet shifting on the black and white marble floor. She looked older, more mature, more like a woman and less like a girl. She held her head with confidence even if her features betrayed her true feelings. He could see the concern playing out on her face. She had noticed his injuries. How could she not have?

"And I—I missed you too," she said with shaky smile. "I didn't think you would be coming home so soon. Surely you didn't think so either." Her eyes grew solemn.

Oliver nodded, wishing he could hide his face from her somehow. She must have thought him unsightly and pitiful. She, on the other hand, looked perfect. How did she manage to look perfect even when her bonnet was askew and her face was flushed? He wasn't certain if that perfection was in her appearance, or simply in his eyes, but whatever it was, he had missed it. He had missed her more than anything else he had left behind. Yet he couldn't bring himself to say it. In his absence, she must have spent two seasons in London. Even if she didn't have a child, he still would be mad to even consider the possibility that she wasn't yet married. He coaxed his hopes back to their rightful place.

He cleared his throat. "Before you say another word, come to the drawing room and sit by the fire. You must be freezing. I'll have a tea tray brought in." He set Rupert down on the marble floor before walking to Julia's side. The butler offered to take her cloak.

Oliver took the opportunity to study her face again, his heart pinching. He looked away. He could hear their countless conversations, endless laughter, and hours of childish mischief in the back of his mind. He led her away from the open door where the cold air had begun drifting inside. Rupert followed closely on his heels, exhibiting far more energy than a dog his age would be expected to possess.

The fire in the hearth was already burning, so Oliver simply pulled a chair forward for Julia, motioning for her to sit. He then dragged a second chair across the Persian rug until it was beside hers. She was watching his every motion. He could feel her gaze on the side of his face—the side with the ghastly, haphazardly stitched cut running from his eye to his jaw. When he met her gaze, she looked away, staring into the fire instead.

"Why did you walk here?" he asked when the silence grew uncomfortable.

"It was easier and less dangerous to walk in the snow than it would have been to travel by coach. It's a walk I've made many times." Her eyes flickered to his. If he could read what was playing through her mind, he likely would have seen the same memories that were playing through his own. How many hundreds of times had Julia or Oliver taken the path between their two homes?

His heart sank as he considered the fact that she had taken the walk without a chaperone. Only married women could be considered proper in doing so. The intensity with which that thought tortured his heart made him aware—more aware than ever—of his feelings for her. They had persisted through years and miles, and in his absence they had even grown stronger.

Rupert whined at his feet, pulling Oliver from his thoughts. He scooped up the old dog, setting him in his lap. He had once been able to make the jump from the floor to a chair with ease, but that seemed to have changed over the past two years. Similarly, he and Julia had once been able to make conversation with ease. It felt different now.

"I find it curious," Julia began, eyes fixed on Rupert rather than Oliver, "that you thought I was holding a child."

Oliver's face grew warm. "Any sensible person would have thought the same. Most women do not carry their dogs bundled inside their cloaks to keep warm."

"Well, I couldn't return him to you half-frozen." A slight smile touched her lips, but she still fiddled with her skirts nervously. "I had to show you that I took proper care of him in your absence. You were right to trust me with him, though I confess I will miss him a great deal."

"I won't allow you to miss him," Oliver said. "You are welcome to come see him any time you like." The thought of Julia frequenting the drawing room at Larkhall rose his spirits more than he had expected.

She smiled. "I would like that very much."

He hesitated. "You might bring your family with you as well. Are you…or any of your sisters…married?" He held his breath. He had only asked about her sisters so she wouldn't think he was too interested in her marital situation specifically.

Julia's eyes rested on his. "No. Not yet."

Had she emphasized the word *yet*? Even so, a flood of relief washed over his shoulders. *Not yet* was a better response than *yes* would have been.

Julia moved her gaze to the floor, warming her hands by the fire. "My mother has plans to see me engaged to a man by the name of Lord Belper."

Oliver's stomach dropped. "But you are not yet engaged?"

"No."

He swallowed, fighting against the dread climbing his throat.

"And if it were up to me, I would choose never to become engaged to him. He is ridiculous." She glanced up. "But my parents cannot afford another season for me. I confess I have not taken my other seasons seriously enough, and so my mother is now trying to convince me that I will never receive another offer."

Oliver felt his heart flip in his chest. If it wouldn't be absurdly shocking, he would have made her an offer that very moment.

Rupert shifted on Oliver's lap, planting his front paws on Oliver's chest and sniffing his face. Before he could be stopped, Rupert licked the length of Oliver's cheek—right over his wound. He flinched, leaning back in his chair.

Julia's brow knit with concern. "Does it hurt?" she asked in a soft voice.

"Not so much now."

She nodded toward his hand, which was wrapped up tightly, hiding the ghastly wounds from her sight. "What happened to your hand?"

A memory surfaced in his mind. One day, just a few months before Oliver had left for sea, he and Julia had sneaked out of their houses together unchaperoned, though it was improper to do so alone once Julia was out in society. They hadn't cared. They had gone to their favorite bridge near the edge of Larkhall's property. They often sat with their feet hanging just above the stream, throwing pebbles into the water. There had been no point to it, aside from spending time together. In October, the woods were cold, and the water colder. After throwing a handful of wet pebbles into the stream, Julia had complained of cold fingers. Oliver hadn't thought of the consequences of warming her hand in his. He had touched her hand many times before, briefly, accidentally, but he had never held it. Sitting on the bridge, he held her hand for several minutes, even after it was warm again. The smile she had given him in that moment was one he could never forget. He remembered looking down at their entwined fingers and commenting about how small hers were in comparison to his. The top of her fingertips barely reached the base of his top knuckle.

But now two fingers were missing on that hand—his left hand—the one that Julia had held that day by the stream.

It took him a moment to remember that Julia had asked him a question. She was likely imagining all kinds of ghastly injuries hidden beneath the wrappings. "My hand was hit by a musket fire and I lost two fingers," he said. "My other injuries were caused by glass and wood fragments from the cannonballs that struck our ship." He didn't want to look at Julia's reaction. His embarrassment had come not only from the fact that he was missing fingers, but that he had come home injured and not victorious.

"I'm sorry you went through such a horrible experience." Julia's voice was heavy. "But I am glad to see you again and that you are alive. I am certain Rupert feels the same."

Oliver nodded, offering a small smile. "Thank you for looking after him while I was away."

"Well, he was once mine, after all." She met his smile with one of her own. Hers was shy and a little mischievous. "Do you remember how he came into your possession all those years ago?"

Oliver had never forgotten it. His smile grew. "I am surprised you are not too embarrassed to remind me."

Even as he said it, her cheeks darkened. "Well, I am not expecting you to take that marriage agreement seriously. It was obviously never valid. As a child I believed it was, but we both know it isn't." She laughed awkwardly, looking down at her feet.

Oliver shifted in his seat. "Of course not."

"I would never hold you to it, even though I am turning twenty-one this month." She kept her gaze fixed on her boots.

On Christmas day. Oliver had always celebrated Julia's birthday with her, sneaking away from his family's Christmas festivities in order to see her.

He studied her unreadable expression as she avoided his gaze. Even if the bargain they made as children was valid, and that letter he had signed had bound him to her, Julia wouldn't want to marry him now. He had failed in his career. He was now deformed, and without the sort of large income that

Lord Belper or many other eligible men could give her.

"As you said, it isn't valid." He shrugged, trying to maintain his smile. "But it is an amusing memory all the same." His heart fell when she gave an abrupt nod.

"Yes. How silly we both were." She stood with a weak smile, brushing a few droplets of water from her cloak from where the snow had melted. "Well, I should be going now. Do not be surprised if I return soon to visit Rupert." Why wouldn't she look at him? Had he said something wrong?

Oliver stood, crossing his arms. Her words, *to visit Rupert*, rang in his ears. She wouldn't be coming to visit him, just the dog. He pushed the vexation from his mind. "Julia—do not walk home. I will have a carriage prepared."

She paused, considering the idea for a long moment. "Very well. That is very kind, thank you."

Oliver's mood was horribly somber as he left the drawing room with Rupert at his heels. He tensed his jaw, surprised by how much pain enveloped him. Even if Julia didn't want to marry him, he needed to stop her from marrying a man she didn't love. He couldn't bear the thought of her being unhappy.

Her birthday was approaching, and if he was going to treat it as any other birthday of hers, he would need to give her a gift. This year, rather than a traditional gift, he would give her something much more helpful and lasting. Determination rose in his chest as he limped his way to the courtyard. This year, as his gift to Julia, he would do all he could to save her from a marriage to Lord Belper. It wasn't for his own benefit. No, his reasons were entirely selfless. It was a birthday gift, nothing more.

One he would happily give.

CHAPTER 4

Julia stirred her soup rather than eating it that night at dinner. She stared at the candles flickering at the center of the table, ignoring her mother's voice for the second time.

"Julia?" Mama said in a clipped tone. "Why are you so distracted this evening?"

Julia looked up from the candles, swallowing the emotion that had been rising up in her throat all day. "I am not distracted." Her voice was too defensive.

Mama exchanged a glance with Elise and Jane, her two younger daughters, before taking another bite of her soup in silence. She dabbed at her lips with a serviette. "You cannot fool me, my dear." A furrow marked her brow. "Are you thinking of Mr. Northcott and his injuries?"

Julia shook her head as quickly as she could. "No. I miss Rupert, that is all."

"I see." Mama's lips pressed together in a frown. "You knew the dog was only yours temporarily. You should not have allowed yourself to grow so attached to him."

He was not the only one she had allowed herself to grow too attached to. Her heart stung as she thought of the curt tone with which Oliver had agreed that their old contract was entirely invalid. Of course it was, but she had hoped he might still consider it. It didn't matter that it was invalid if he *wanted* it to be valid. But instead, he seemed to think the idea ridiculous. She was nothing more than a friend to him, just as she had always been. *That* was why she was distracted, but she could never tell Mama.

"How is Oliver faring?" Elise asked. She sat with perfect posture as she ate her soup without slurping. She would make a fine debutante. She was beautiful and accomplished and kind, and her heart was free for the taking, unlike Julia's had ever been.

How *was* Oliver faring? He was less cheerful than he had once been. He was more reserved. That was to be expected given all that he had endured. "He seems to be faring well considering his circumstances."

"Bringing Rupert to him surely raised his spirits," Elise said. "Surely seeing you raised his spirits as well."

Julia hadn't told a single soul besides her old friend Mary of her love for Oliver. Not even her sisters knew how she had pined for him when he was away. She couldn't reveal her feelings now after she had become so skilled at hiding them. "It was wonderful to see such a dear friend again."

"We should invite the Northcotts to our Christmas Eve ball," Mama said. "And," she added between bites, "we will ensure Lord Belper is there to dance with you, Julia. I suspect he is very close to a proposal."

Julia nearly groaned aloud in dismay, but she stopped herself. There were still two more courses to be served; she couldn't argue with Mama this early on in the meal. "Yes, we must certainly invite the Northcotts." She chose to ignore the second part about Lord Belper. "They are a very amiable family."

"Indeed." Mama drank from her goblet, eyes sparking with delight.

Julia stared at the candles again, grateful when Mama turned the subject of conversation to Elise, and then Jane. Julia hoped her sisters would never experience the pains of unrequited love.

She stopped her thoughts before they could go too far astray. Whether Oliver loved her or not was not her most pressing concern. She needed to find a way to stop Lord Belper from proposing, or she would never have a chance to see if Oliver could come to love her with time. If Lord Belper proposed, Julia would be forced to accept him. Mama would have it no other way.

"Perhaps we should not wait until Christmas Eve to see the Northcotts," Mama said. "I will invite them to dinner on Thursday along with our other guests. I plan to have our greenery hung a few days early this year rather than waiting until Christmas Eve. We will have more time for people to come admire it."

Would Oliver even accept the invitation? She wanted to see him again, and she couldn't risk the disappointment of him not coming to dinner. Perhaps he was ashamed to be seen in public with his injuries, or in too much pain to leave his house.

Julia took a bite of her soup, absentmindedly slurping. Mama shot her a look of dismay, but she ignored it. She was distracted yet again. If she wanted to see Oliver, she would have to take matters into her own hands.

Julia had only taken ten steps toward Larkhall and she was already tempted to turn back. She missed *Rupert*. Not Oliver. She was visiting Larkhall in order to see her favorite dog in the whole world, not her favorite person in the whole world. That was what she told herself, though she wasn't certain if she believed it. Three days had passed since she had returned Rupert to him, and she wanted to know how he was adjusting to his previous life at Larkhall.

She watched her feet as they made prints in the snow. The air was clear that day, without a single snowflake falling. The snow underfoot had become thick, causing each footfall to make a crunching noise. Watching her feet rather than her other surroundings was essential. She refused to slip and fall in front of Oliver again.

Another set of crunching footfalls make her pause. She stopped walking, and the crunching continued. So it hadn't been her own feet.

She looked up from under the wide brim of her bonnet. Down the path, Oliver was walking straight toward her. Even since she had seen him a few days before, his limp seemed to have improved. He held the end of a leash that was secured around Rupert's neck. The dog seemed to have caught sight of Julia, picking up his pace. His breathing was labored as he tugged against the leash around his neck to reach her.

"Oliver?" Julia said. She walked toward him with slow steps. He wore a smile of disbelief as Rupert continued to tug at the leash with strength that defied his age. Why did she feel so nervous around Oliver? Meeting him here by chance made her more flustered than she cared to admit.

Rather than looking up at his face again, she stooped down to scratch behind Rupert's ears. "I was just on my way to visit you," she said, speaking more to the dog than to Oliver. She straightened her posture, daring a look at Oliver's face.

His smile remained, and it tied her heart in a knot. "I was on my way to visit you as well," he said.

"Truly?"

"Rupert insisted." Oliver nodded toward the dog.

She grinned. "Is that so? Have you taught him to speak?"

Oliver gave a serious nod before his expression melted into another smile. Julia had always loved how his smile transformed his face. He was even more handsome with it than without it. His blond hair was combed neatly today, his square jaw clean shaven. The cut on the side of his face had healed a little more since she had seen him three days before, but it still looked painful. Her heart stung for him.

"The only words I have taught him to say are your name and mine," Oliver said. "He simply wouldn't stop speaking your name, so I assumed that meant he wished to see you again."

"Ah, I see." Julia laughed. "But I'm afraid you are giving yourself too much credit. I was the one who taught him to speak your name long before I brought him back to you. He has been saying it every day for the last two years."

"Well, it seems he cannot choose his favorite. Perhaps he cannot be without either one of us." Oliver's smile softened. Could he have been thinking the same thing Julia was thinking? If they were ever married, then Rupert could be with them both. They really ought to marry one another. Purely for the poor dog's sake.

"How are matters with Lord Belper?" Oliver asked.

Julia's stomach twisted. There was nothing in Oliver's tone to indicate that he resented the man who would soon propose to her. She needed to stop with her dreaming and scheming. "Nothing has changed." She sighed. "He called upon me yesterday, and I was quite afraid he would propose. Thankfully, he didn't yet." She had tried to keep Lord Belper's visit brief, but he had brought several poems to read to her and it had taken over an hour.

Oliver was silent as he turned back toward Larkhall. Between their two houses, Larkhall was closer. They walked for several seconds before Oliver spoke, kicking the snow in front of him with the tip of his boot. "If he does propose…do you plan to reject him?"

Julia certainly *wanted* to reject him, but to do so would be foolish. He was rich, respected, and titled. A match with him would do wonderful things for her family, and Mama would likely never forgive her for rejecting him. If there was no hope for Oliver, then what reason could she have for not securing a comfortable future for herself and her eventual children? She couldn't be a romantic any longer. It had only served to hurt her.

"I don't think I can reject him," Julia said with a sigh. "Mama would be devastated. With no other offer, I would be destined for spinsterhood. I cannot slight a man of his social standing, and I have come too far in our courtship. Everyone already assumes there is an understanding between us. If he proposes, I will have to accept." She examined Oliver's face as he walked. He seemed to be thinking deeply about something.

He finally met her gaze. "What if he never proposes?"

She exhaled through her lips. "That would be wonderful, but I'm afraid it is unlikely."

"Unless I help you make it more likely." He raised one eyebrow.

Julia caught the glint of mischief in his eyes that she had always seen when he was younger. Her heart hammered. What did he mean? Would he propose to her instead? Attempt to steal her away from Lord Belper? The romantic side of her that she had been suppressing came out of hiding. "H-how would you do that?" she asked in a careful voice.

Oliver smiled. "It would not be entirely up to me to stop him from proposing, but I could help you learn to repel him."

"Repel him?"

He nodded. "I will befriend him myself and discover everything he dislikes in a woman's conversation, conduct, and appearance, and you must implement each one. If you repel him successfully, he will not propose and you will be free of your obligation."

Julia stared at him as her confusion grew. It was as if he had already planned this entire thing. It hadn't been as romantic as she had hoped, but another thought struck her. Why was Oliver so interested in ensuring that she didn't marry Lord Belper? Hope sparked in her chest.

And so did a little mischief.

"What will happen after Lord Belper decides not to propose to me? Shall I accept a life of spinsterhood? Why should I willfully deter my one and only suitor?" Julia watched his reaction carefully.

Oliver must have learned many skills during his time aboard that ship. He had never been able to hide his feelings from his face before, but now he was an expert. "He won't be your one and only suitor," Oliver said. "Your mother is wrong to think that. After your courtship with Lord Belper is over, then you will be free to find a man who you actually love." He looked down at Rupert, which seemed to be both of their tactics when they felt uncomfortable. "I will even help you find him if you wish."

Nothing sounded worse than Oliver Northcott helping her find a husband. He must have truly never cared for her at all if that idea didn't vex him like it vexed her.

"Very well," she said, walking with her arms crossed. "I do like the first part of the plan." She wouldn't hide that she wasn't fond of the other part. "It will not be easy, I'm afraid. For some reason, Lord Belper seems quite determined to like me."

Oliver smiled, casting her a sidelong glance. "I can think of many reasons he would like you."

Julia's heart stammered, but she chose to ignore it, clapping her hands together abruptly. "Well, how shall we begin?"

They walked up the front steps of Larkhall and

inside the grand doors. Julia removed her hat, gloves, and cloak before following Oliver to the drawing room. He stopped when he reached the door, pausing to listen to the voices within. "That is my mother, Bridget, and Matthew," he whispered. "It might not be wise to discuss our plan with them listening."

This was just like when they were children, always up to one scheme or another, hiding from their families. Oliver returned her smile in the dim hallway, and it made her heart leap all over again. "Did you receive my mother's invitation to dinner tomorrow?" she asked.

Oliver nodded. "We will all be there."

"As will Lord Belper," Julia said. "You can befriend him that night and discover what might deter him." She kept her voice as quiet as possible.

"I will take my duty very seriously." He leaned just a little closer, and a thrill raced over her spine. She didn't feel that way when Lord Belper whispered and smiled.

Julia had thought their words were quiet enough, but Oliver's mother must have heard something. The drawing room door opened, and Mrs. Northcott peeked her head out. "Julia, is that you?" A smile split her face. "It has been too long." Her cheerful voice and expression had always reminded Julia of Oliver. Mrs. Northcott ushered them into the drawing room. "I was happy to see the invitation from your mother, but I didn't think I would have the joy of seeing you prior to dinner on Thursday."

"It is wonderful to see you as well." Julia smiled.

Matthew, Oliver's elder brother, and Bridget, his younger sister, sat on the sofa. As small as she was, Bridget's feet hung above the ground, swaying back and forth with delight when she saw Julia. Her blue eyes brightened. Matthew offered a bow and smile in greeting, and the smile seemed to hold a series of questions. His eyes darted between Oliver and Julia, his lips curving steadily upward.

Julia's face flushed just a little to have been discovered whispering in the dark corridor with Oliver, but the Northcotts had a way of putting anyone at ease. Already, in the few days since she had seen Oliver, he seemed more at ease himself. She was beginning to see glimpses of how he had been before his injuries had sent him home.

She drank tea and ate ginger cakes with the Northcotts, speaking of light, happy things. Julia was overly aware of how close Oliver sat to her on the settee, but she tried her best not to dwell on it. If she hoped too much, she would be disappointed. She couldn't allow herself to hope that he returned her feelings, nor could she allow herself to hope that he might propose to her instead of Lord Belper. Such a thing wouldn't even be possible unless she first repelled Lord Belper with Oliver's help. She was going to succeed. She had to. Because—as far as she was concerned—she had a prior engagement.

CHAPTER 5

Mrs. Reeves, Julia's mother, stared at Oliver's face for a long moment when he entered the drawing room at Reeves Manor. She didn't hide the shock in her expression as her eyes traced over the gash running from the corner of his eye to his jaw. Almost instantly, her gaze jumped to his hand, still bundled in bandages. Perhaps he should not have been so eager to attend a social event until he had healed, but the matter was urgent. He had a lofty task ahead of him. To convince a man not to be in love with Julia seemed impossible.

His heart skipped with admiration when he saw Julia, dressed in a soft pink evening gown, standing in the corner of the room. Her golden hair was arranged without a strand out of place, contrary to how it had been the last two times he had seen her out in the wind and snow. He liked how she looked both ways—refined as well as reckless. But the one thing he didn't like about her appearance that evening was the obviously fake smile on her lips.

Already, Lord Belper had engaged her in conversation, practically trapping her against the wall.

He started in her direction, but Julia's mother stopped him. "Oh, Mr. Northcott, you must be in a great deal of pain." Mrs. Reeves, to her credit, seemed genuinely kind and concerned, not disgusted by his injuries.

"The pain is manageable, I assure you. Thank you for your invitation. It has been too long since I've been in this house." He gave a polite smile before making his way farther into the room. Matthew and his mother had already found a gentleman and lady to converse with. The group was small, consisting only of Oliver's family, Julia's family, the couple that Matthew was speaking with, and of course, Lord Belper.

Oliver had never met the man before. He was not as bad looking as Oliver had hoped, though he did seem to be a great deal older than Julia. His rapt attention was fixed on her, even though Julia's eyes were darting at anything but him. Her gaze landed on Oliver, with a look that said, *rescue me*.

He immediately crossed the room, coming to a stop beside them. He bowed to Julia before turning toward Lord Belper. Julia gave their introductions, clasping her hands together nervously behind her back.

Though Oliver was already not fond of the man, it

was his duty to befriend him this evening. That was the essential first step of the plan. He put on his most charming, cheerful smile. "You must tell me where you purchased that waistcoat," he said to Lord Belper. "I've never seen such a fine cut of fabric."

The man looked down at his waistcoat, his billowy cravat partially blocking his view of his own chest. He flattened his cravat with the palm of his hand to get a better glimpse. Then he smiled, shrugging one shoulder. "I am not excessively fond of it myself. I do not particularly like the color blue. It is just a little too close to green for my liking." He gave a quick, high-pitched chuckle. "I despise green."

Oliver met Julia's eyes in a fleeting glance. "I never cared for it either," Oliver said. "It truly is a hideous color."

Lord Belper gave an emphatic nod. "I am glad to finally have found someone who shares my opinion on the subject! Green never improves the appearance of anything. I much prefer red or pink." His eyes slid to Julia, who happened to be wearing a pink gown. She shifted uncomfortably under his watchful gaze. He licked his lips before turning back toward Oliver.

Julia absolutely could not marry this man. How could she have even been considering it? Her family's influence did hold a great weight, but she needed to trust her own heart. It was clear that her heart did not, and never would, belong to Lord Belper. Oliver did all he could to keep the man's attention off of her as they waited in the drawing room before dinner. Julia seemed relieved to have Oliver nearby. He spoke with Lord Belper about every subject the man seemed most interested in speaking of, agreeing with nearly every word he said, encouraging his ideas in his attempt to win his favor.

When they walked to the dining room, Oliver wasn't surprised that Mrs. Reeves had seated Julia directly beside Lord Belper. Oliver sat beside Matthew, eating each course of the meal while answering the questions directed at him about his time at sea. He met Julia's gaze across the table several times throughout the meal, and each time, he was reminded of how lovely she looked in pink.

Lord Belper was right about one thing.

When the ladies left the dining room, Oliver stayed behind with the men for port. They poured their glasses, and Oliver practiced his questions in his mind. In his earlier conversation, he had discovered many things about what Lord Belper liked. But most importantly now, it was time for him to learn more about what Lord Belper *didn't* like.

Julia sat on one of the settees in the drawing room, tapping her gloved fingers on the book on her lap. She had successfully left the space beside her open in the hopes that Oliver would claim it when he came back to the drawing room. She needed to hear what he had discovered about Lord Belper. Despite the fact that her mother was watching all of their interactions, she would have to implement what Oliver learned as soon as possible. At any moment, it could be too late and Lord Belper would be requesting a private audience with her to offer his proposal.

The drawing room door opened, and Matthew entered first. Then came the other gentleman in attendance, Mr. Golding. Behind him, conversing as if they were the dearest of friends, was Oliver and Lord Belper. Matthew sat down by his mother, Mr. Golding by his wife, and Oliver and Lord Belper both started toward that one empty space beside Julia on the settee.

She swallowed, staring at Oliver with wide eyes as he allowed Lord Belper to take the seat. She sighed under her breath, picking up the book on her lap as quickly as she could. Was this part of Oliver's plan? Was he giving her an opportunity to begin deterring him? She had tried before without any success. She needed a new tactic, and only Oliver could help her with that.

But he was now sitting on a chair near the bookshelf —too far away to help her.

She threw him a questioning look. Why hadn't he raced Lord Belper to the seat beside her? Oliver met her gaze before turning toward the books on the shelf beside him. "Julia, would you care to help me choose one? I haven't done enough reading of late."

Julia held his gaze for several seconds. What was he

doing? She kept her expression smooth as she tried to read his. "Of course." She stood, starting in his direction.

The other guests were engaged in their own conversations, leaving Julia and Oliver's interaction less noticeable. As she walked toward Oliver, she prayed Lord Belper wouldn't follow her. Thankfully, he remained seated, though she could feel his gaze on her back.

Oliver turned to face the shelf, and Julia did the same. He picked up a book, holding it out in front of them. He then lowered his voice to a whisper, one almost undetectable among the other voices in the room. "He despises Mozart's sonata eleven, particularly the third movement. I recall that you once knew it." He flipped the pages of the book, meeting Julia's eyes briefly before looking away again casually.

Julia nodded, fighting a smile. "I do know it. I shall play it tonight."

"That is a start, but not enough. Do not only play it." Oliver looked up. "Explain to him how it is the only piece of music you ever play. Tell him you play it at least ten times a day, and that you plan to do so for the rest of your life." The mischievous gleam in Oliver's eyes combined with his smile made Julia's heart soar. Oh, how she had missed this side of him.

She held back her laughter. "Ten? I play it twenty times at least. Day and night when I cannot sleep."

"Even better." Oliver lifted the book closer to his

face, pretending to read from the page. The curve at one corner of his mouth was impossible to miss.

Julia walked back to Lord Belper's side, avoiding his searching gaze. When it came time for musical performances, she turned toward Lord Belper. "I am going to play my very favorite piece. I have practiced it twenty times a day for the last several years, and I will continue to do so for the rest of my life." She repeated the words she had practiced with Oliver. "One can never truly master anything."

"That is true dedication, Miss Reeves." Lord Belper grinned. "I find that quite admirable. What is the piece?"

"Mozart's eleventh sonata."

His face fell.

She turned away, eagerly awaiting her mother's call to the pianoforte. She rose when she was invited to the seat, playing the piece from memory. It was rather convenient that Lord Belper hated a song she had practiced so much. It was one of her favorites. When she finished the piece, she returned to her seat.

Lord Belper stared at the floor, mouth a firm line, eyes wide. He wiped a bead of perspiration from his forehead. "You are very talented, Miss Reeves. Is there… any other song you enjoy just as much?"

"No. I am committed only to that particular piece. I refuse to learn any others." She gave him a warm smile. "I hope to soon increase my repetition of it to thirty times daily. I never grow tired of it."

"Thirty?"

"Yes, thirty, my lord."

Julia exchanged a glance with Oliver but looked away quickly enough to stop herself from laughing.

Lord Belper hardly spoke a word to her for the rest of the evening, which was a welcome change of events. He still complimented her upon taking his leave, but his voice was not convincing. His eyes didn't linger on her quite as long as they usually did, and his smile only stretched half as wide.

Oliver passed Julia on his way out, bidding his farewell to her mother, and then turning back to her again. He looked to both sides as if to ensure he wouldn't be overheard. "Well done," he whispered.

"Thank you." She smiled, brushing her curls away from her forehead. "I don't think Lord Belper was pleased with my performance."

"Did I mention that Mozart's eleventh is my favorite?" Oliver kept his voice low.

"Is it?"

He nodded, a hint of a smile on his lips. "The piece has always reminded me of you." His eyes connected with hers.

Julia's stomach fluttered, jerking one way, then the other. How could one simple look cause such a disruption? Only Oliver had ever been able to have that effect on her. "I did practice it often. That much was not a lie." She paused, composing herself again. Being so close to him was doing strange things to her heart. He might have looked a little older and a little different with the cut running down the side of his face, but his eyes were still the same. Her very heart was reflected in them, just as it always had been.

"What else shall I do to repel him?" she asked in a whisper. "What other things did you learn about him?"

He glanced at her mother, who had begun observing their conversation. "Pay a visit to Rupert and me tomorrow." His voice was quick.

"I will."

Oliver nodded and offered a bow in departure, keeping his expression even. Julia watched his back as he took his leave of the room. She wiped the smile off her face the instant Mama returned to her side. All the guests were gone. Julia's sisters still sat in the drawing room, giggling over how handsome Matthew Northcott was, and how handsome Oliver was, despite that he would always have a scar over his face. Julia didn't even see the scar. All she saw was his heart, the same heart she had always loved.

"That Oliver Northcott is a good man," Mama muttered. She met Julia's gaze with a weak smile. "It is unfortunate that he doesn't have more to offer."

She walked away without another word, leading her other daughters out of the room to prepare for bed. Julia stood in the empty space, listening to the ticking clock.

Mama would never understand.

Oliver could offer Julia far more than any man

could. He would offer her happiness, joy, and love. None of that could be compared to the wealth and status that Lord Belper could offer her. She would trade everything she possessed to know that she had Oliver's heart and that he could be hers forever. If only he would make such an offer.

Heart aching, she turned and made the walk to her bedchamber.

CHAPTER 6

Oliver could have made the entire situation much easier if he proposed to Julia himself. He sighed as he set Rupert on his lap, scratching the dog behind the ears with his unbandaged hand. He had been sitting around like a fool all day, waiting for Julia's arrival. He should have called upon her instead. What had he been thinking? She would likely walk to Larkhall in the snow as she had the first time. He had only waited because he didn't know if they would have the opportunity to speak privately at Reeves Manor, especially with her mother watching her every move.

He debated for a few more minutes before securing a leash around Rupert's neck and leading him outside toward the path that led to Reeves Manor. The snow had begun melting in some places, but was hardened on the surface in others. Oliver's boots crunched through the icy snow, but Rupert's paws kept him lightly atop the surface.

Surprisingly, just as he reached a patch of trees, Julia walked through, arms crossed, watching her feet as she had been the day before. She must have been on her way to visit him as they had planned.

"A green cloak?" Oliver said, making her jump. "Lord Belper would disapprove."

Her eyes flew to his, wide with surprise. She laughed. "I am simply practicing for the Christmas Eve ball tomorrow."

Oliver smiled at the redness of her cheeks and the wry smile on her lips.

"So it seems you take Rupert on many walks." Julia nodded toward the dog in question.

Oliver laughed. "Well, I decided I didn't want to make you walk all the way to Larkhall in the cold. I planned to walk to your house, but it seems I am too late."

"This is better, isn't it?" Julia asked, adjusting the ties on her cloak. "We may discuss our mischievous plan in secret out here."

"You're right." It was very improper to do so, and Oliver knew Julia's mother would be fit to be tied if she knew, but at the moment, he didn't care. If they were caught and any scandal was assumed, he would simply have an excuse to offer to marry her without fear of being rejected. Though that was not ideal either. He wanted Julia to love him. He suspected that she had cared for him once, but that had been a long time ago, long before he had failed at his career and lost his fingers. He looked down at his bandaged hand without intending to.

"I know the perfect place," Julia said, starting toward the trees. Discussing their secret scheme out of doors out in the open was one thing, but hiding among the trees to do so was another. There were any number of people who could pass through and find them there, likely to assume scandal.

But, like a puppy, Oliver followed her. "Where are you going?" he asked.

Julia walked quickly, and the elderly Rupert struggled to keep up.

She didn't travel far before stopping beside the stream with the bridge that she and Oliver had sat at countless times. She turned around with a smile that made his heart stutter. "Do you remember this place? It is only fitting that we discuss our plan here." She walked onto the bridge, sitting on the edge and dangling her feet over the partially frozen water.

Oliver joined her, holding Rupert in his lap. "How long can we last before we freeze?" he asked.

"I would wager only a few minutes." She reached for the dog, pulling him toward her and wrapping him up in her cloak. He turned, sniffing her face as she laughed. She wriggled away from his face as he tried to kiss her. "Perhaps less if Rupert continues to be so affectionate."

Oliver would have loved to have been the one who

was being so affectionate. He laughed at the dog, but he was envious of him at the same time. One of the last times Oliver had sat here with Julia, he had held her hand. Did she remember that day? Had she thought of it as frequently as he had?

She met his gaze, eyes bright with inquisition. "So…tell me what else you discovered about Lord Belper."

Oliver crossed his ankles where they dangled off the edge of the bridge. "Many things. As it turns out, he despises more things in life than he likes. He made my task quite easy." He looked down at the stream before glancing at Julia again. He should have sat on the opposite side of her. From her place, she had a clear view of the long cut on his face. It must have been unsettling to look at.

But if she was unsettled, she didn't show it. Her smile persisted. "Soon enough, I will be at the top of that list of what he despises," she said.

Oliver chuckled. "That is what we should hope for. But I do have doubts about our success. I think it is nearly impossible for anyone to despise you."

A hint of color touched her cheeks. Did that happen when Lord Belper spoke to her? He didn't think so. Perhaps she did still have some feelings for Oliver, but she was simply just as afraid to acknowledge them as he was.

"Fortunately, we know that wearing green will make me instantly despicable. Wearing my green gown to the ball will be essential," she said, tapping her chin. "But what else might I do?"

Oliver reached toward Rupert and covered his ears before saying, "Lord Belper despises dogs."

Julia gasped, then grimaced. "How dare he. A man who despises dogs is quite possibly the most unattractive sort."

"I know. It is atrocious." Oliver grinned, uncovering Rupert's ears. The dog's large brown eyes blinked up at him with surprise.

"How might I use that information to my advantage?" Julia raised one eyebrow.

"You might explain to him how you wish to raise three dogs alongside your children, treating them as additional members of your family."

Julia covered her mouth, eyes wrinkled at the corners with a smile. "Perhaps I play my favorite piece by Mozart to each of my dogs, one by one, as they go to sleep at night."

"Perfect."

"While wearing my favorite green nightdress, of course." She leaned toward him, laughter garnishing each word she spoke.

"He also mentioned that he hates the smell of Rosemary," Oliver said. "In his words, 'it makes him gag and retch.'"

She gasped. "I think my mother has a bottle of Rosemary perfume. I will spray the entire thing all over myself."

Oliver had nearly forgotten the subject of their conversation. All he could think of was how relieving it felt to laugh again, and especially to laugh with Julia. He hadn't realized how much he had missed the sound of her laugh.

That reminded him. "He also despises when a woman's laughter is too high-pitched."

"Is my laughter high-pitched?" she asked, brow creasing.

"No." Oliver almost touched her hand to reassure her, but he stopped himself. "Your laugh is perfect."

She met his gaze for a brief moment before her lashes shielded them from view. "Do you think all of that will be enough?"

"If it isn't, you might also bring up the subject of your favorite food, which you must tell him are cucumbers. He told me that there is nothing he despises more than cucumbers."

"Because they are green?" Julia asked, one eyebrow raised.

"What other reason could there be?"

She laughed again, and he joined her. She turned toward him fully, a hint of concern replacing her jovial expression. "Hopefully my mother doesn't recognize my scheme."

"You will be subtle enough, so long as you keep your conversations with Lord Belper private."

"Thank you for your help," she said in a quiet voice. She looked down at Rupert, a shy expression cloaking her face. "If we succeed, I shall be free to marry when and whom I choose."

Oliver looked down at the water. Would she marry him if he asked? He was not the same as he had once been. And he would never have the wealth and title that her mother hoped for her to secure. He felt Julia's gaze on the side of his face. Did she want him to reply? What could he say? His thoughts were interrupted by the sensation of Julia's fingers against the skin on his cheek. He turned to look at her, shocked by the gesture. A shiver followed the movements of her fingertips, racing down his neck and spine. Her brow was furrowed as she traced the length of his cut with her gaze and fingers. When she met his eyes, she gave a soft smile. "I think it quite suits you." She lowered her hand from his face, but he could still feel it there.

His heart pounded, his doubts fading. She hadn't been disgusted by the scar on his face as he had suspected.

"And your hand," she said, draping her fingers softly over his bandages, "it will only serve to showcase your strength and bravery. No one will think less of you for it. Especially not me." The sweetness of her words spread warmth through his chest.

Before he could think of a reply, she stood abruptly, handing Rupert back to him. "I ought to be going home." She shivered, and he detected another hint of shyness in her features. She had never touched his face before, but he would take it as encouragement. "Thank you again, Oliver. I will see you at the ball."

"I will be there," he said, rising to his feet. Their eyes locked with a weight he couldn't explain, and he almost abandoned his resolve to keep his feelings hidden. All he wanted to do was keep her there with him a while longer, no matter how cold it was. Offer her his heart, kiss her, secure her hand in marriage before Lord Belper could even dare to try. But, like a coward, he couldn't manage to find the words. "W-we shall see if our efforts meet success."

"I believe they will." Julia gave another small smile before turning toward the path that led back to her home. Oliver watched her go, his heart lighting on fire. Even if they didn't succeed with deterring Lord Belper, he couldn't simply stand by and assume that she would never marry him. Perhaps she was waiting for him to realize that she would say yes.

He banished his hopes before they could rise too high. The first step was to put a stop to Lord Belper's advances, then he could consider the second part of his plan.

Rupert was staring at the footprints in the snow that Julia had left as she walked away, tail wagging.

"I know," Oliver muttered to the dog. "I love her, too."

CHAPTER 7

Julia twirled in front of the looking glass, examining each angle of the dark green taffeta gown she wore for the Christmas Eve ball. Her maid had arranged her hair in an elegant coiffure, lifting all her blonde curls off of her neck, aside from a few framing her face.

Though her greatest task of the evening was to repel Lord Belper, she had found her thoughts more occupied by how she could manage to secure Oliver.

She would have time, of course, once Lord Belper was successfully deterred. Mama would stop pressuring her to marry that odious man, and she could be free to spend more time with Oliver. Eventually, he might develop feelings for her that matched what she felt for him.

She bit her nail nervously before putting on her

gloves to stop the horrible habit. Why was Oliver so difficult to read? He had been acting like a brother, or a protective friend, but there were moments when she sensed more between them. But it might have just been her hopes playing tricks on her.

Turning back to the mirror, she picked up the bottle of Rosemary perfume and sprayed it on her arms, bodice, neck, and hair until it ran out. She coughed at the strength of the smell, grinning at her reflection. That should do it.

With her chin held high, she walked down to the ballroom where the guests had already begun gathering. It wasn't a large dancing room, but it was large enough for their party. Greenery and gold ribbons had been hung in all directions, candles sparkling and casting shadows on the polished floors. Julia walked inside, searching the crowd for Oliver.

She caught sight of him standing across the room, arms folded, fingers still bandaged. He looked handsome with his black jacket and white cravat, his hair appearing more golden under the candles and gold ribbons. He met her gaze, and a smile tugged his lips upward. She walked toward him, and he walked toward her until they met somewhere in the middle.

His eyes washed over her, a hint of admiration in them. Had she imagined it? She did all she could to hide her nervousness. "Have you seen Lord Belper?" she asked.

Oliver's soft blue eyes remained locked on hers. "I saw him by the refreshment table."

"How shall I begin our plan?"

"He is likely to ask for a dance," Oliver said. "You know the subjects to bring up that will most deter him." He breathed deeply through his nose as a grin curled his lips. "And he will be sure to smell that rosemary even from his place all the way across the ballroom."

Julia laughed, covering her mouth with one gloved hand. "Is it too much?"

He breathed in through his nose again. "Oh, it is certainly too much, which is precisely what we wanted. However, I happen to like the smell of rosemary. And," he drew just a little closer, a smile still lingering on his mouth, "I think you look lovely in green."

Her heart leaped, and she checked his expression for any sign that he was only teasing. There were no signs. Had Oliver just…flirted with her?

She didn't have time to dwell on it. Lord Belper had spotted her, and he was making his approach. Oliver retreated to the outskirts of the ballroom, wishing her luck with a smile.

From the corner of her eye, she watched Lord Belper weave his way through the crowd. He stopped when he was just a few feet away. His legs came to an abrupt halt. He seemed to take a moment to compose himself, his nose wrinkling with distaste. He walked closer, staring at her gown with growing displeasure.

"M-miss Reeves, how do you do this evening?" His nose was still wrinkled. The rosemary must have been even stronger than Julia had thought. Already, a sheen of perspiration glowed on his brow, making the dark curls stick to his skin.

"I am quite well. How are you? Is something amiss?" She raised her eyebrows, keeping her expression serious.

"There is a certain…aroma." He cleared his throat in what might have been a gag.

Julia gave the high-pitched laugh she had been rehearsing, to which he responded with wide eyes. "You must be smelling my perfume. It is my favorite. I use a great deal of it, so I ran out, you see. I was finally able to purchase a new bottle today. Now I'll be able to resume wearing it every day."

Lord Belper adjusted his cravat. "Ah. Perhaps you should use a little less of it." His eyes were still examining the green fabric that she wore.

"Why should I do that? I adore the smell of rosemary."

His upper lip curled as he met her gaze again. His throat bobbed with a swallow.

"Did you enjoy the refreshment table?" Julia asked in an innocent voice.

Lord Belper seemed to shake himself of his distractions for a brief moment, though his nose was still wrinkled. "Yes. In fact, I might return there for a drink of water."

Perhaps he truly was going to vomit at the smell of her.

"While you are there," she said, "will you look to see if there are any cucumber sandwiches? Cucumbers are most refreshing in a hot ballroom. I did already eat my breakfast cucumbers and my luncheon cucumbers, but I can never have enough of them."

Lord Belper's eyes rounded even more. He walked away in silence, muttering under his breath.

Julia exchanged a glance with Oliver, who stood near enough to overhear their conversation. It was going quite well. He seemed to be suppressing a smile, but he did well to hide it. She took a deep breath, relieved to have a short break from her act.

When Lord Belper returned, he held a small cucumber sandwich on a serviette, staring at it as if it might sprout legs and lunge at him. Julia took it and ate the entire thing in one bite. "I feed my dogs cucumbers," she said, wiping her lips with the serviette. "They love them as much as I do."

"Dogs?" Lord Belper raised his eyebrows. There was more perspiration on his brow than there had been before.

"Oh, yes. Have I not mentioned them? They are housed in the stables here at Reeves Manor. Three large, strong hounds. I adore them. They are like children to me. I shall never be separated from them." She sighed in contentment.

The first dance was soon to begin, and Lord Belper was growing more pale and sweaty by the second. He gave a very fake, stiff smile before offering a slight bow. "Well, then, Miss Reeves. That is very nice." He inhaled sharply, nose wrinkling again. He looked down, taking a step backward. He was silent for a long moment. "I hope you enjoy the rest of the ball."

Julia gave a polite smile. "You as well." She could hardly believe her luck when Lord Belper crossed the ballroom and asked a different young lady for a dance. Julia watched as he escorted her to the center of the ballroom, his grimace still present.

Oliver stepped up behind Julia, his voice close to her ear. "That was perfection. You should be an actress." Laughter hovered in his voice.

She turned around, stifling a giggle of her own. "I cannot believe it worked so easily. My mother was certain he was in love with me."

Oliver shook his head slowly, holding her gaze for a long moment. "Love is not as fickle as that."

Her stomach flipped.

"Since Lord Belper failed to claim your first dance, may I?" he asked. The question was light, but his eyes were heavy and intense. It stole her breath.

Her words were suddenly evading her, even after she had just spoken so many ridiculous ones to Lord Belper. So instead of speaking, she nodded, following Oliver to the line of dancers.

The music led them into a slow rotation, stepping

together, stepping apart. Her hand touched his as they turned, and then broke away. The music was slow, plucking at her heart, as if the musicians had somehow chosen it as their primary instrument. She listened to the music that came from her heartstrings, the whisperings she had come to recognize so clearly. They told her again and again what she already knew—she loved Oliver. His eyes bore into hers, gentle and strong at the same time. Reliable and safe. She could hardly breathe with each brief touch, wishing each moment could last longer. She held Oliver's bandaged hand gently, hoping to somehow assure him that it did not scare her. He was whole and perfect in her eyes, and he always would be.

Their dance ended, and Oliver's chest rose and fell with a heavy breath. He met her gaze with a smile, one that she returned without any reservation.

They returned to the side of the room, and Oliver soon asked her for a second dance. The next was far more exhilarating, a lively tune with rapid steps. She laughed until she could hardly breathe. She had always wanted to dance with Oliver. It was something she had dreamed of as a young girl, and now it was happening. He was smiling as she hadn't seen him smile since returning from sea, and it was utterly contagious.

When the song ended, she walked with him again. She had to hold one hand to the back of her drooping hair arrangement to keep it in place. Oliver laughed, leaning toward her. "One more dance and it shall be completely undone."

She already was undone. Every last stitch holding her back from pouring out her heart to Oliver had been clipped. She was feeling strangely confident and brave. Her heart pounded.

A hand tugged on the back of her arm, interrupting her thoughts.

Julia turned around. It was Mama. Her blonde curls were tight on her forehead, and her teeth were displayed in a fake smile. Her hand grew tighter around Julia's upper arm. "May I have a word, my dear?"

Julia glanced back at Oliver before nodding, following Mama into the corridor. The air was colder and darker, and the voices from the ballroom became muffled. The moment they were out of sight of the guests, Mama let out a huffed breath. "Why is Mr. Northcott claiming your dances and not Lord Belper?"

Julia shrugged, twisting a loose thread on her glove. "Lord Belper has not shown any interest in me this evening. Oliver has." She lifted her chin. "And I am quite happy with the situation."

Mama sighed, rubbing her forehead. "I know you have always cared for Oliver as a *friend*. But don't you see that your endeavors would be better focused on securing a match of higher rank? On someone with more to offer?"

Julia shook her head, her throat tightening. "No one has more to offer me than Oliver. He is a good man, with a good heart. He makes me laugh and smile. He understands me. I have never loved, nor will I ever love anyone more. He offers me happiness, and that cannot be matched with any measure of wealth or status." She caught her breath, holding Mama's gaze.

She had expected Mama to argue, but instead, the stern lines of her face gave way to a soft smile. "I suppose he still does have a very influential family, even if they are without titles. I didn't know you felt so much for him. Does Oliver know how you feel?"

Julia shook her head. "No."

"Perhaps you might encourage him a little," Mama suggested with a smile. "If both of you carry on silently loving the other, then nothing will ever become of it."

"I don't *know* if he loves me." Julia looked down at the floor, heart pounding.

"Then you ought to ask." Mama tucked her fingers under Julia's chin, lifting her eyes to hers. "If Lord Belper is no longer interested in you, perhaps it was fate intervening."

It wasn't quite *fate* that had driven him away, but Julia would keep the truth of it to herself. Mama was far less upset than she had expected. She cast Mama a grateful smile, heart beating wildly against her ribs. How could she possibly ask Oliver how he felt about her? How could she tell him how she felt? It had been so many years of hiding her heart from him. But he must have known to some degree. She had, after all, tried to trick him into marrying her all those years ago.

"For now, enjoy the rest of the ball," Mama said. "Do not fret. All will be as it should be." She turned to walk away, but stopped, sniffing the air. "Are you wearing my old perfume? How much did you apply?" She grimaced.

"Far too much, I'm afraid." Julia bit her lip before hurrying past Mama in order to escape further questioning.

Oliver was waiting near the wall when she returned to the ballroom. Seeing him after her conversation with Mama set her heart pounding all over again.

His brow was knit with concern. "Is everything all right?"

Julia nodded, hiding her nervousness. There was no hurry to confess her feelings to Oliver. The bravery she had been feeling moments before had vanished. "Yes. I resolved her concerns."

"Good." Oliver drew a deep breath as he looked down at her. He paused for several seconds. "Tomorrow is your birthday."

"My twenty-first," she said, fiddling with her glove again.

"At the age of twelve, I assumed that birthday would never come," Oliver said with a chuckle. "But now here it is upon us. Funny, is it not?"

He was referring to that silly agreement they had made. According to the rules, he would be bound to marry her after tomorrow came and went. But it was invalid. Ridiculous. Completely unfounded.

Oliver took a deep breath like he wished to say more, but he held the breath instead, eventually releasing it. If neither one of them were ever brave enough to voice their feelings, then they would remain as they had always been. Friends.

And simply being friends with Oliver was not enough anymore.

CHAPTER 8

Pacing in front of his bed had never solved Oliver's problems like he hoped. He stopped, sitting down on the edge instead, raking a hand through his hair. It was Christmas day and Julia's twenty-first birthday. He wanted to see her now that Lord Belper was out of the way. He wanted to tell her how he felt…how he had felt for years now. The emotions were bottled in his chest, and the pressure was torturing him.

He had a perfectly reasonable excuse to call upon her that day, with it being her birthday.

He needed to give her the gift he had been planning.

But that was the part that made him the most nervous.

Stop being a coward, Oliver ordered himself. He had been planning his gift all night. But he had hardly slept as he had tried to plan the words that would accompany the gift. He took a deep breath, tugging on his boots and starting toward the door. Greenery had been hung all around the corridors of Larkhall, and Oliver could smell the spices of Christmas dinner wafting through the air from the kitchen. If his gift was well received, then he could return and enjoy the holiday without the turmoil and nervousness raging inside him.

When he reached the ground floor, his mother walked around the corner, one hand pressed to her chest. He had expected a more cheerful expression on her face, considering that it was her favorite day of the year. He stopped in his tracks. "What is it?"

Mother's brows drew together with concern. "Oh, Oliver. I am so very sorry. I-I opened the door this morning and didn't see your little Rupert. He ran outside as fast as he could, and I don't know where he has gone."

Oliver's stomach dropped. It was cold, and Rupert was not young. He could very well lose his way and freeze. He didn't waste a moment. "I'll go look for him." He darted toward the door, heart racing.

He limped out to the frost-covered grass, scanning the area frantically. Where could he have gone?

Scratch.

Scratch.

Julia approached the back door of Reeves Manor slowly, brow furrowed.

Scratch, scratch, scratch.

The sounds continued. Something was scratching at the door from the other side. It might have been a tree branch…if not for the fact that there were no trees near the door.

And if not for the fact that the scratching was accompanied by a familiar bark.

Julia tugged the door open. As she had suspected, Rupert stood on the other side. He looked up, tail wagging as he waddled into the house. He shook his coat, sending flecks of snow in all directions. Circling Julia's heels, he barked again.

"Rupert! What on earth are you doing here?" She bent down to scratch behind his ears. Did Oliver know his dog had come here? There was no leash attached to his neck. "Did you escape? That is a very naughty thing to do."

Rupert barked again in response.

Julia scooped him up, carrying him to the drawing room, where the yule log was burning in the hearth. The additional warmth combined with the scents of the greenery helped to settle Rupert down. Julia held him on her lap as she sat in one of the chairs near the fire. Should she return him to Oliver? She bit her lip. Since the ball the night before, she had been nervous to see him again. What was he thinking now that he knew she had no obligation to Lord Belper? Was it now up to her to encourage him and hint at her feelings? She couldn't very well declare them first, but how could he doubt them? Her mind raced as she stroked Rupert's wet fur.

A knock came on the front door, jerking her out of her thoughts. She jumped to her feet, inching closer to the drawing room door. The butler's voice echoed in the entryway, welcoming *someone* into the house. The moment the guest spoke, she recognized his voice.

It was Oliver.

Julia held Rupert tightly—perhaps too tightly—as she made her way to the corridor. "Oliver?" she called as she walked around the corner. He was standing just inside the front doors, hair mussed, out of breath, and covered in snowflakes. He laughed when he saw Rupert, wriggling in Julia's arms. The tip of his nose was pink, and his eyes shone with delight when they settled on Julia. Her heart thudded against her will.

"I knew he must have come here. He escaped this morning." He strode forward. But rather than focusing on the dog, his eyes were still focused on her. His gaze was gentle and cautious. "It seems that Rupert wanted to come wish you a blessed birthday and happy Christmas." Oliver smiled, and the expression nearly melted her. "As do I."

How did he manage to look so endearing covered in snow? A smile overtook her face. Without thinking, she reached up to brush the bits of snow off his shoulders and chest. "Thank you," she said in a quiet voice. Her hand froze, and she quickly whisked it away from his chest. She held his gaze for a long moment. "You-you should come to the drawing room and warm yourself by the fire."

Without waiting for a reply, she turned around and began walking in that direction. Her breath came quickly, and her legs shook beneath her. Why was he making her so blasted nervous? She could hear his footfalls right behind her. She set Rupert on the floor, and he led the way to the warmth of the drawing room. He curled up by the fire, watching intently as Oliver entered the room behind Julia.

"He is very content here," Oliver said, stopping near the pug and the fire. He lifted his hands to warm them, glancing over at Julia. "It's quite coincidental that Rupert came here of his own accord." He paused. "I, well…I planned to give him to you as a birthday gift."

Julia's jaw dropped. "You would give him up?" Her heart ached. She had given that dog to Oliver so long ago. By returning him to her, it felt like he was confirming that he would never marry her. She was twenty-one now, and he might have felt some sort of obligation to give the dog back. She stared into the fire, struggling to form the right words. Her throat tightened with sudden emotion. "Oliver—you don't have to give Rupert back to me." She blinked back a tear that hovered at the edge of her eye. "Is this because I'm twenty-one now? We have already discussed that the contract I made was invalid. You need not feel any sort of obligation toward me. You may keep Rupert, and I will not hold you accountable for our bargain." She sniffed, losing control of her composure as one tear escaped. All the years she had hoped to marry Oliver—all those wishes and thoughts she had spent on him—felt like they were dying in front of her. They were shriveling up and burning in that fire with the yule log.

She couldn't look at him. He had been silent for too long.

"Julia—" he drew a heavy breath, stepping toward her. She looked up in time for him to touch the side of her face, cupping it in his hand. Her eyes rounded in surprise as he moved in front of her. His touch sent a string of shivers over her skin, and her heart nearly stopped. It took her a moment to realize that he was shaking his head. "You are wrong. Even if we had never made that contract, I would still be standing here today. I'm not here to give up Rupert. I'm here with the hope that I can share him with you."

"Share him?" Julia blinked, trying to soak in the words. She was utterly distracted by Oliver's fingers burying in her hair and his thumb caressing her cheek. His meaning became clear as she looked up at his eyes, blue and wide with sincerity. They traced over each feature of her face, settling last on her lips. A slow smile curved his own.

"Do you not understand what I mean?" he asked, a

mischievous gleam in his eyes. "Was it not your objective all along?"

Her hands curled at her sides, and she could hardly manage to draw a breath. Longing cascaded through her in waves, each one growing more intense than the last. Hope sprung in her chest, but she didn't dare guess his meaning. She didn't want to be wrong. Her heart pounded so hard it hurt. "Do you think I planned to have you and Rupert both one day? How could a girl at the young age of eleven concoct such a scheme?" Her voice was breathless as he leaned closer.

"Only Julia Reeves could be so clever." He brushed a curl from her forehead. "And only I could be such a fool. I have been a coward, helping you repel Lord Belper rather than just propose to you first myself."

She stared up at him, eyes wide. Her hands grasped his lapels, and she rose on her toes. "Do you mean it?" Her voice cracked.

Oliver pressed his forehead to hers, hooking his other arm around her waist. "I want to marry you, Julia."

She pulled back enough to see his eyes, those same eyes she had shared countless glances with, so many unspoken words. She could hardly believe the words that had just escaped his lips—those same lips she had shared countless smiles with. How could it be true? Her joy was spilling over, and she nearly threw her arms around him. Her vision flooded with tears, making Oliver's face a blur. "Are you being serious?"

"Yes," he said in an exasperated voice. "I love you. I have for a very long time."

Julia laughed as a tear rolled down her cheek. Her vision cleared and his smiling face came into view again. "I love you, too. I always have."

Oliver wiped away the tear on her cheek, his gaze lowering to her mouth. She held her breath as he traced the curve of her lower lip with his thumb. Her throat was raw as he leaned down, brushing his lips against hers with far too much caution. She was through with being cautious. She slid her hands inside his jacket and around his waist, capturing his lips with hers in one concentrated motion. She pulled him as close as she possibly could, transforming his tentative kiss into the one she had been dreaming of for years. With her permission granted, Oliver's response was immediate. His fingers buried in her hair, and his kisses abandoned their gentleness. Her skin erupted with shivers, and her legs shook beneath her as he kissed her again and again. She ran her fingers over his hair and the melted snowflakes in it, and he wrapped his arms around her waist. His lips slowed to playful, soft caresses, until he pulled back, leaning his forehead against hers. "Do you accept my proposal?" he murmured, tracing his thumb over her cheek again.

Her lips tingled from his kiss, her heart still thudding a quick rhythm in her chest. "Yes." It had never been easier to answer a question in her entire life. It had always been Oliver. She had been wise enough to see that from a very young age, and she could hardly believe she had nearly given up hope. If anything was worth waiting for, it was a love like the one she felt now, surrounding her with as much warmth and security as Oliver's arms.

She sighed, smiling up at him. "We have already been engaged for ten years, after all."

LARKHALL LETTERS SERIES

A Prior Engagement is a prequel novella to the Larkhall Letters series. Find the complete series on Amazon!

Larkhall Letters Series
The Ace of Hearts
The Captain's Confidant
With Love, Louisa
The Matchmaker's Request
Lord Blackwell's Promise

ABOUT THE AUTHOR

Ashtyn Newbold grew up with a love of stories. When she discovered Jane Austen books as a teen, she learned she was a sucker for romantic ones. Her first novel was published shortly after high school and she never looked back. When not indulging in sweet romantic comedies and regency period novels (and cookies), she writes romantic stories of her own. Ashtyn also dearly loves to laugh, bake, sing, and do anything that involves creativity and imagination.

Connect with Ashtyn Newbold on these platforms!
  INSTAGRAM: @ashtyn_newbold_author
  FACEBOOK: Author Ashtyn Newbold
  TIKTOK: @ashtynnewboldauthor
  ashtynnewbold.com

Printed in Great Britain
by Amazon